OF SHADOW AND MOONLIGHT

OFFICIAL COLORING BOOK

LUNA LAURIER

ISBN 9781962409063 (Paperback)

Illustration Credits

Huangja : Pages 5, 7, 9, 11, 13 , 15, 17, 19, 21, 23, 25, 27, 29, 31, 33, 34, 35, 37, 39, 41, 43, 45, 47, 49, 51, 53, 55, 57, 59, 60, 61, 63, 65, 67, 69, 71, 73, 75, 77, 79, 80, 81, 83, 85, 86, 87, 89, 91, 93

Vhexi: Pages 4, 6, 7, 8, 10, 12, 14 ,16, 18, 20, 22, 24, 26, 28, 30, 32, 36, 38, 40, 42, 44, 46, 48, 50, 52, 54, 56, 58, 62, 64, 66, 68, 70, 72, 74, 76, 78, 82, 84, 88, 90, 92,

The text in this work originally appeared in Of Shadow and Moonlight © 2022 and Tipped in Frost and Blood © 2023

Book Design by Luna Laurier

OF
SHADOW
AND
MOONLIGHT
OFFICIAL COLORING BOOK
LUNA LAURIER

I'll be right back, Cas. It's gonna be okay." Mom's voice was as soft and reassuring as she could muster, but it did little to fill the void in my chest. I'd almost worked up the courage to tell her I'd attend today's checkup on my own, but she'd been so eager for possible good news that I hadn't had the heart to turn her down.

So, once again, I'd bent.

How long before I broke, though?

The door clicked loudly as it closed behind them, echoing off the walls, and for a moment, I couldn't seem to make my body move. Bland white walls surrounded me, decorated with diagrams of the heart and cardiovascular system. Various tools and odd gadgets sat on display along the counter of a nearby cabinet.

It felt... lifeless.

The things I'd experienced within the walls of a medical facility never truly left me, and while I did my best to act like I was okay, I wasn't. I wasn't okay. I was tired. Tired of hospital trips, needles, IVs, tests. Tired of doctors' offices, the pitiful glances, the bad news, the dead ends. Tired of... the monotony of it all.

—Of Shadow and Moonlight

superior
vena cava
aorta
pulmonary
artery
pulmonary
vein
pulmonary
vein
right
atrium
left
atrium
pulmonary
id
right ventricle
A
B
D
E

His long dark hair spilled in gentle waves over his shoulders as he reached down, hand hovering as he moved to grab my spilled drink. He had the most dazzling eyes I'd ever seen, silvery gray with flecks of rich amber that burst from the center, popping against his deep olive skin. I could imagine myself drawing the lines of his face, his jawline, the dark stubble dusting his skin, bridging over his lips.

He sat frozen for a moment as our eyes met, a subtle look of shock on his face. "How—" He cleared his throat before he blinked and attempted to compose himself. "I'm so sorry, let me… let me buy you new drinks."

—Of Shadow and Moonlight

IGN'S

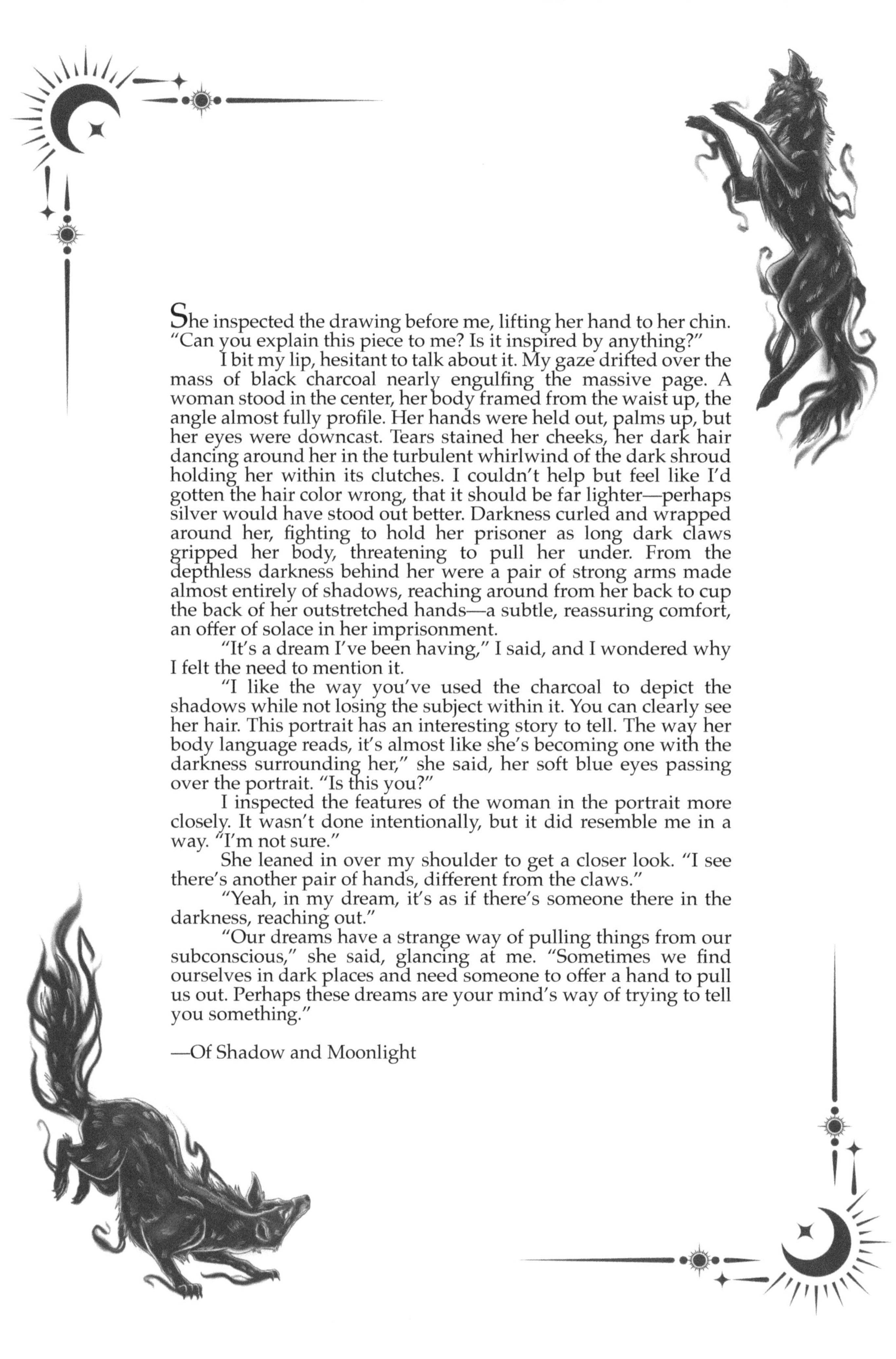

She inspected the drawing before me, lifting her hand to her chin. "Can you explain this piece to me? Is it inspired by anything?"

I bit my lip, hesitant to talk about it. My gaze drifted over the mass of black charcoal nearly engulfing the massive page. A woman stood in the center, her body framed from the waist up, the angle almost fully profile. Her hands were held out, palms up, but her eyes were downcast. Tears stained her cheeks, her dark hair dancing around her in the turbulent whirlwind of the dark shroud holding her within its clutches. I couldn't help but feel like I'd gotten the hair color wrong, that it should be far lighter—perhaps silver would have stood out better. Darkness curled and wrapped around her, fighting to hold her prisoner as long dark claws gripped her body, threatening to pull her under. From the depthless darkness behind her were a pair of strong arms made almost entirely of shadows, reaching around from her back to cup the back of her outstretched hands—a subtle, reassuring comfort, an offer of solace in her imprisonment.

"It's a dream I've been having," I said, and I wondered why I felt the need to mention it.

"I like the way you've used the charcoal to depict the shadows while not losing the subject within it. You can clearly see her hair. This portrait has an interesting story to tell. The way her body language reads, it's almost like she's becoming one with the darkness surrounding her," she said, her soft blue eyes passing over the portrait. "Is this you?"

I inspected the features of the woman in the portrait more closely. It wasn't done intentionally, but it did resemble me in a way. "I'm not sure."

She leaned in over my shoulder to get a closer look. "I see there's another pair of hands, different from the claws."

"Yeah, in my dream, it's as if there's someone there in the darkness, reaching out."

"Our dreams have a strange way of pulling things from our subconscious," she said, glancing at me. "Sometimes we find ourselves in dark places and need someone to offer a hand to pull us out. Perhaps these dreams are your mind's way of trying to tell you something."

—Of Shadow and Moonlight

Y ou talkin' about me, princess?" Barrett threw his arm over Cole's shoulder as he leaned in. "I knew you still loved me, Cole."

I stifled a laugh as Barrett made kissy faces at Cole over his shoulder. Cole growled and elbowed him off, the interaction turning into a tussle.

—Of Shadow and Moonlight

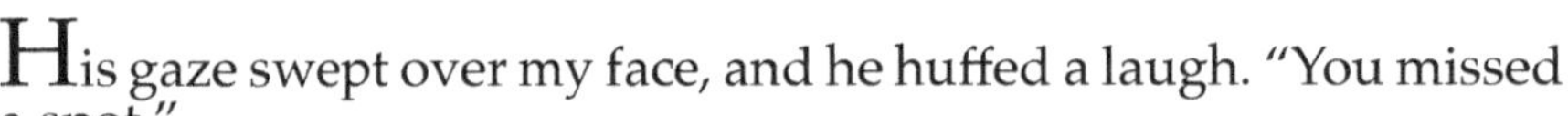

His gaze swept over my face, and he huffed a laugh. "You missed a spot."

His thumb brushed over my jaw, wiping away the remnants of charcoal I'd missed, and I scrunched my face. The strange sensation I'd felt the first time we touched seeped into me where his fingers met my skin, something deep in my chest reaching out to him in response. My heart raced at the feel of it, and he inched closer, so close, until our breaths mingled.

"You're always smiling, but I can't help but feel like there's something else behind those eyes. I can't figure it out, but it almost seems... sad." His voice was low, and I struggled to focus on his words as his body pressed against mine, my back meeting the shelves.

"No matter what I do, no matter how much I try to stay away, I can't stop myself. You're too irresistible..." His hand lingered against my skin, and it slid along my chin, tilting my face up. His voice dropped to a low whisper as he leaned into me, his lashes lowering as his eyes fell to my lips. *So fuckin' irresistible.*

—Of Shadow and Moonlight

Air rushed into my lungs when one of the fleeing men lunged at him, fist raised as he attacked, but the hooded man shifted, clothes-lining the attacker. The guy crashed onto his back, and the shortest of the hooded pursuers surged forward, pinning him down. The pursuer who'd knocked him down jerked the blade over his head.

My heart sank as he plunged the blade into the guy's chest. I recoiled as the most horrendous screech assaulted my ears, my knees buckling as I clamped my hands over my ears. It did nothing, the sound clawing its way into my mind, rattling me down to my bones. As it faded, I shoved to my feet and raced downstairs, nearly falling down the stairwell.

—Of Shadow and Moonlight

Air halted in my lungs as I came to a stop, finding myself face to face with another of the creatures. I froze—this one somehow felt different.

Its face changed, shifting until it more closely resembled a human. Her black hair flowed around her like shafts of pure darkness, fading into smoke that danced and writhed at her back. A disturbing clicking sound slipped from her lips, and other clicks echoed in the darkness around us in response.

Something about the sight of her aroused a strange sensation within me that I didn't quite understand, as if my body was trying to communicate something to me. Her lips parted as she breathed, her razor-sharp teeth glistening. Her hollow black eyes moved over me, as if she was inspecting me. I should be running, but I couldn't pull myself away from her gaze, and I took in the details of her face; the pale gray skin, so shallow that I could see the black web of veins, stretching out from around her eyes, under her neck. Her hand shot out, black-tipped, clawed fingers wrapping around my throat. I gasped, trying to move, trying to fight her off, but I found my limbs unresponsive.

Her icy breath flowed over me, into me. She pulled me closer, our faces inches apart. Those hollow black eyes stared into mine, drawing me into their abyss, and the world spun around us. I couldn't pull away, couldn't fight it...

Did I want to, though?

Whispered voices echoed in my mind, speaking in a language I'd never heard before, and my eyes fluttered, my mind buckling under the press of this creature's will.

—Of Shadow and Moonlight

I cleared my throat, dragging myself back down to reality, and scooted back to lean against the nearest rock as I continued to draw. My eyes flitted back and forth between him and my sketch, my heart fluttering at the soft expression on his face, the warmth filling his eyes as he watched me work. I didn't know how much time passed as I jotted down the details of his face, but I started to lose myself in them. His neck. His shoulders. His chest.

After a moment, I realized that this was my first time working with a male model. His features were so different, the coiled muscles lying beneath the surface of his skin, the veins of his hands. I wondered what he looked like under that shirt. My ears grew hot, and he chuckled.

He sees you, dummy. Stop thinking like that.

—Of Shadow and Moonlight

The sinful combination of his lips and tongue against my skin left me teetering on some sort of edge. When the rush of his hot breath spilled over my skin, it sent a chill through my body, and my legs trembled, heat coiling deep and low.

I wanted more, needed more, and I rocked my hips against him, feeling the brush of his arousal against me, the sensation dragging a breathy moan from my throat. His fingers ground into my hips in the most delicious way, holding me in place, and I shuddered.

He nipped at my ear before whispering, "Easy, *mea luna*. I want to savor you."

—Of Shadow and Moonlight

Just work it together slowly," he whispered. My heart leapt as his chest pressed against my back, and his arms came around to guide mine into the flour. In a steady rhythm, we began working the flour and eggs together, his hands guiding mine.

"See?" he whispered, and I struggled to focus on the dough coming together as we pressed it out before folding it together again. His hands were gentle and guiding, despite how much force we had to put into it. The concoction started to meld together, growing sticky.

"Go ahead and grab a bit more flour," he instructed.

I smiled, reaching out to grab a handful of flour from the spare bowl, and Damien paused to hold his hands out for me to drop some into his palm. He didn't speak as I ran my hand over his, the flour coating our fingers and palms, and he guided my hands back to the dough. The butterflies spun out of control as his presence grew closer at my back, his strong arms brushing against my own as we put our weight into kneading.

—Of Shadow and Moonlight

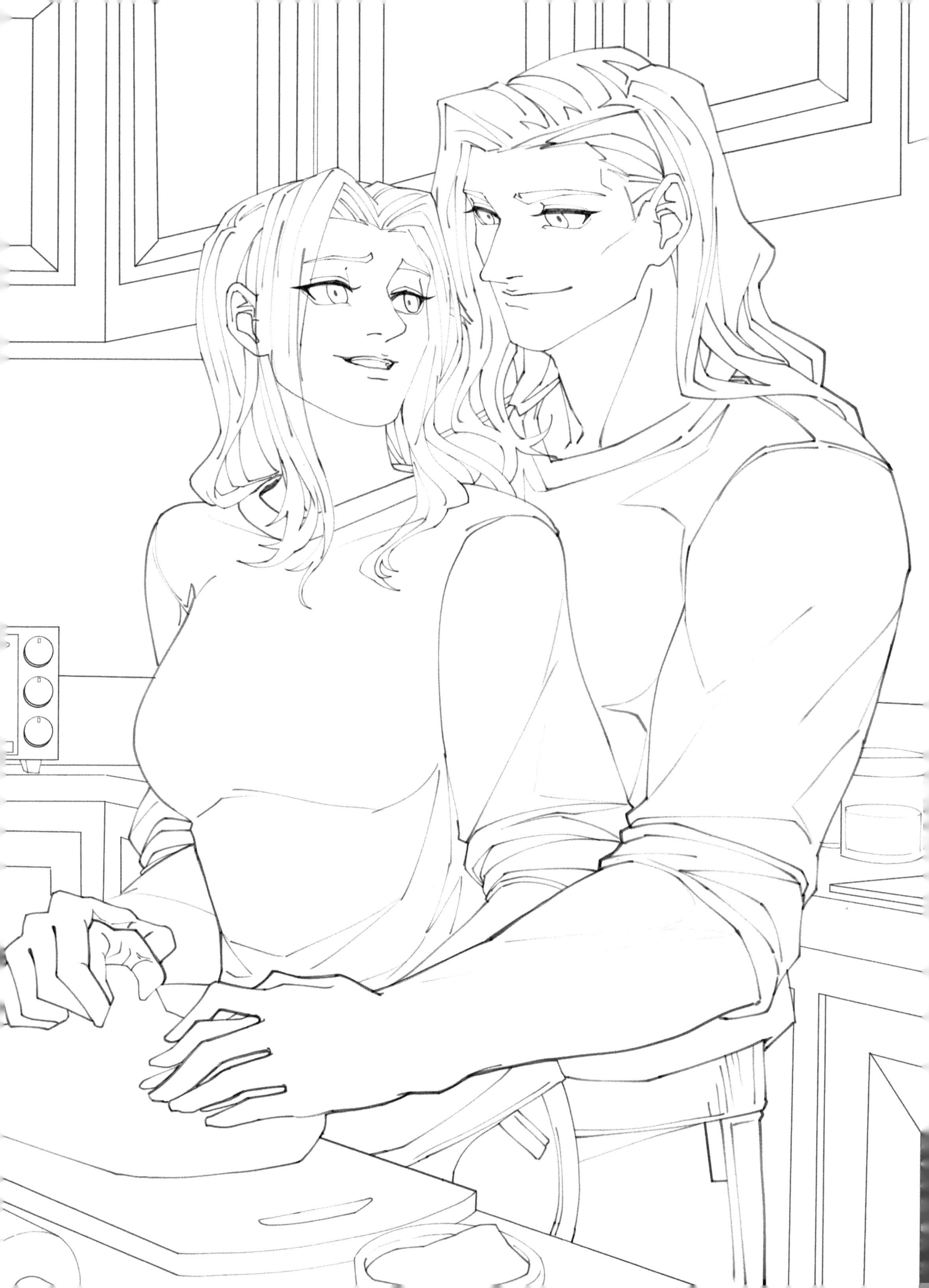

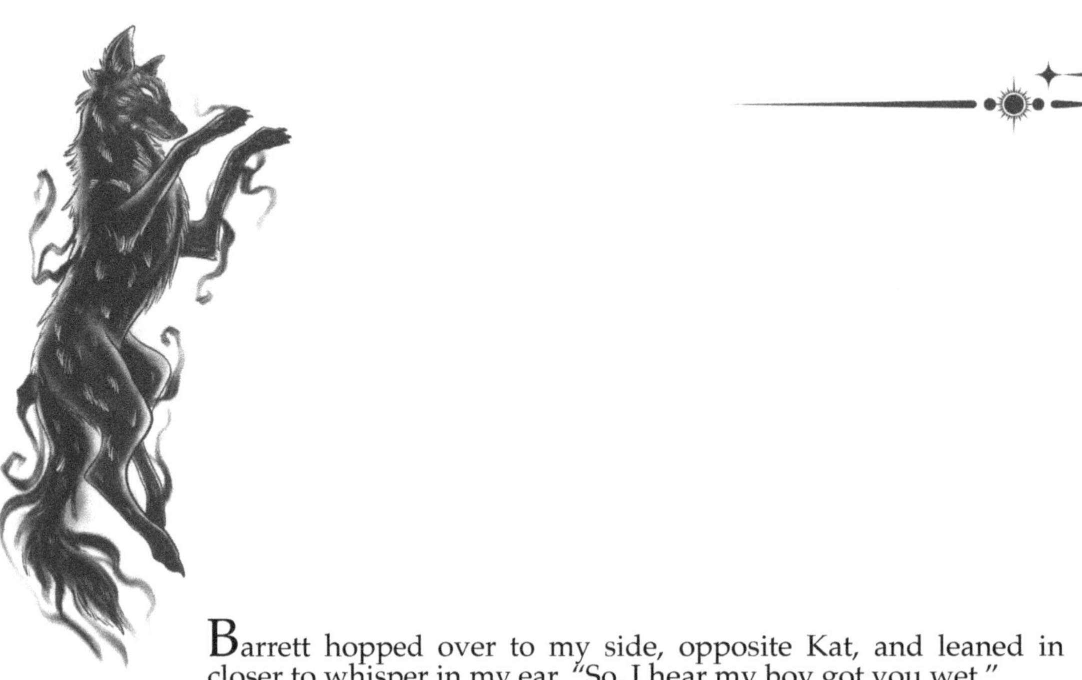

Barrett hopped over to my side, opposite Kat, and leaned in closer to whisper in my ear. "So, I hear my boy got you wet."

The blood instantly rushed to my face, and in that moment, thoughts of Damien and I on his living room floor flashed across my mind. My eyes went wide, and I whipped around instinctually to smack him. Before I could, though, Damien chucked a beer bottle at Barrett, who caught it without taking his eyes off me.

"Cut it out, Barrett. Next time, I'll aim that bottle for your head," Damien warned.

Barrett barked a laugh, popping the cap off the bottle. "I'm just playing, geez! I was talking about her falling in the river." His eyes shifted to me. "Where was your mind going little lady?" His smile turned wicked as I glanced at him. Asshole knew exactly what he was doing.

Kat turned to me. "You fell in the river yesterday?"

Shit. Here we go. I dropped my eyes to the bottle in my hands. "It wasn't a big deal. I'm okay."

She pressed. "Okay, you better get to talking. You promised you'd spill later. It's later."

"Not here." I said, flashing her a look. Her fern-green eyes lit up, and I immediately regretted what I said. She knew something happened between us. There was no hiding it; she knew me too well.

—Of Shadow and Moonlight

An eerie clicking sound echoed around me from the shadows, the sound making my skin crawl. I could barely make out the figures looming in the inky blackness. They stalked closer, creeping up on me now that I was down, like wolves closing in on their kill, their long claws dragging along the ground. I looked up to where the shadows barely concealed more of them, climbing toward me along the brick walls of the buildings surrounding us.

Panic shot through me, and I pushed against the asphalt, desperate to get to my feet. My legs wouldn't obey me, though.

Damien slid to a stop in front of me, arms held out as he stood to defend me. Light barely reflected off the blade of the dagger he gripped as he stared at the creatures.

"Are you okay? Can you stand?" he asked over his shoulder.

I couldn't answer him, couldn't peel my eyes from the demons surrounding us. Their features were the same as the ones I saw in my other dream: gray skin, so thin it revealed the black veins stretching out just under the surface, those hollow black eyes like bottomless abysses, waiting to suck you in with no way of returning. I pushed myself up to stand, but I only made it to my knees.

—Of Shadow and Moonlight

Damien, erase her memory now or I'll do the job myself," Barrett threatened as he drew closer, and the way he said it made it clear it wasn't a threat, but a promise.

How could that be possible, though? How could he erase a memory?

Damien jumped to his feet, turning to stand against Barrett. "Touch her, Barrett, and I swear to the Gods, it'll be the last *fucking* thing you do."

Their eyes locked, a strange electric energy filling the air. When Vincent and Cole moved to intervene, Damien lifted his hand, and they halted, obeying, but lingering on their feet all the same, seemingly ready to stop them. Barrett took a step back, as if some strange understanding passed between them.

—Of Shadow and Moonlight

Zephyr pressed his index finger to my forehead, his lips quirking into a teasing smirk, and something warm filled my chest at the strange gesture. "You keep frowning like that, and you'll get wrinkles on your forehead. It'll be fine, and we'll be back tomorrow."

—Of Shadow and Moonlight

What are you doing?" I asked him, propping a hand on my hip.

Hands grabbed me from the shadows and my heart stuttered as a scream peeled up my throat.

The guys busted out laughing, and I twisted around at the sound of Barrett's own laughter at my back. I elbowed him, and he grunted before recoiling away from me, stumbling against the alley wall, holding his sides.

"You asshole! That's not funny!" I looked back to Damien, who immediately quieted, biting his lip.

—Of Shadow and Moonlight

07:34
BARRETT

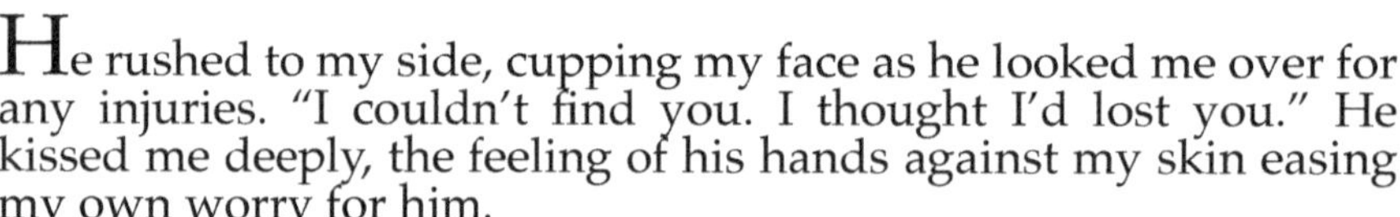

He rushed to my side, cupping my face as he looked me over for any injuries. "I couldn't find you. I thought I'd lost you." He kissed me deeply, the feeling of his hands against my skin easing my own worry for him.

He was safe. He was alive. I couldn't form words as he released me, his hand falling to my stomach, swollen under my leather armor, before he dropped to his knees to press a kiss to it.

"Thank the Gods you're both all right."

—Of Shadow and Moonlight

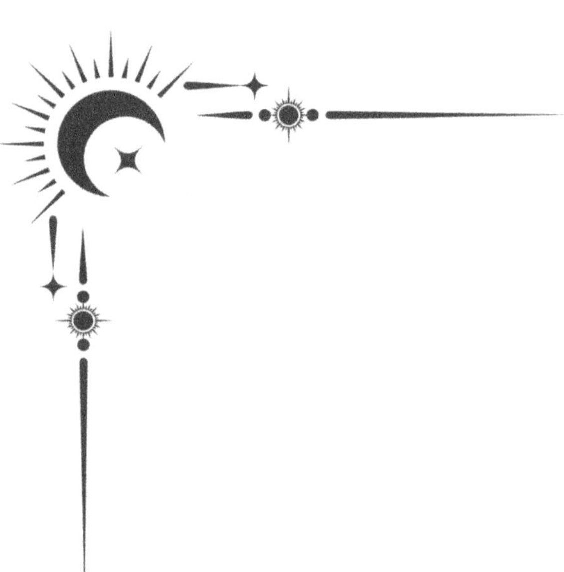

I groaned as my head hung forward, my bones aching from sleeping on the concrete all... night? Was it day? Was it still night? I didn't know how long I'd slept, but it didn't feel like long with the level of exhaustion still clinging to me.

Lights pierced the darkness, bright and blinding, and I closed my eyes, turning my face to try and escape the burning sensation. I cracked my eyelids, trying to get a view of my surroundings, my vision so blurred, all I could make out were shapes and movement.

The room was barren, surrounded by what looked like unfinished concrete walls. Was I in a basement? There were four people in the room I could make out. Someone crouched before me, and as my eyes adjusted and focused, I could see it was Marcus.

He was shirtless, loose cargo pants hanging around his hips, his bare, muscular chest covered in a tattoo that reached over to his arm. Faintly beneath it, though, I could see that it covered an older tattoo, and I couldn't help but think it was similar to Damien's.

—Of Shadow and Moonlight

*F*ight him.

My own voice echoed in the darkness of my mind, bitter and venomous. Only, I hadn't thought it, hadn't thought much of anything over the last few... days? Weeks?

I didn't respond, *couldn't* respond. My skin tingled, as if someone were watching me. Was I not alone? Hands slid over my shoulders as a presence pressed into my back, the voice slithering into my ear. I couldn't turn to whoever spoke, could do nothing but stare forward into the inky, endless void.

He'll return.

The presence faded at my back, and, as if I were looking in a mirror, my reflection rippled into view before me. The form solidified, my features becoming clearer, but something was wrong—a darkness touched at my features. My skin was palish, dark veins stretching out from my eyes, up my neck, branching out down my arms. My reflection leaned in toward me, lips curving into a grin that was all too dark, and she lifted her hand to tilt my chin up, forcing my gaze to meet hers.

When he does, bite back.

—Of Shadow and Moonlight

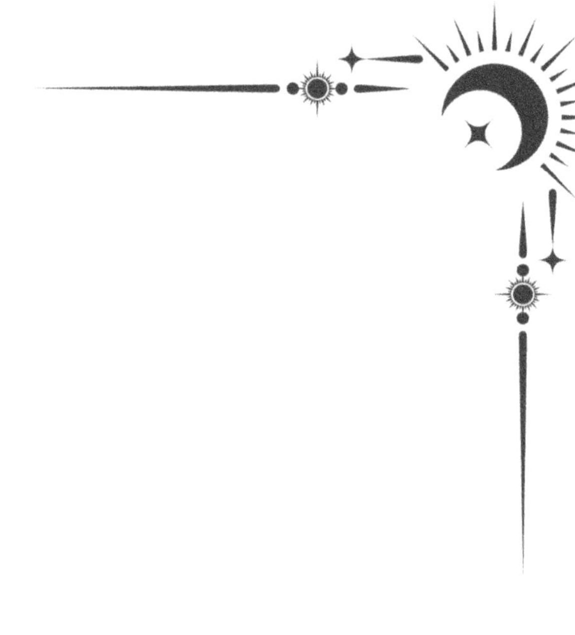

Don't come any closer!" Cole snapped, backing us against the wall. I froze as the icy touch of his knife met the skin of my throat, and I stopped breathing.

Zephyr, Vincent, and Barrett all stopped short at his threat, halting their approach. Damien, though, stepped in front of them, his eyes locked on Cole. Cole's hand twitched suddenly at his advance, and I winced as the blade nicked my skin.

—Of Shadow and Moonlight

Damien wrapped his arms around me, lifting me from the bed, holding onto me tightly, as if his grip alone could tether me to this world. The life began to fade from my body, like a wave receding from the shore.

His agonized voice poured into my ear as he held me. *"I can't lose you, not again."*

"I love you… *mea sol.*" The words floated on what little air I had left.

"Please, stay with me," he begged, holding me tightly. I wanted to stay, wanted to hold the sweet babe whose little face I hadn't even been able to see, but I couldn't hold on any longer.

He pressed his forehead against mine as I gave into the exhaustion, my eyes fluttering closed.

—Of Shadow and Moonlight

Pay attention, Elena!" Damien demanded as he stepped forward, swinging the sword down on me.

Instinct took over, my body moving on its own, sword rising to meet his in the air to stop his blow. He shifted, sliding the blade down before turning it to move past my block. I dodged and stepped back as he advanced, moving the blade to deflect each blow he made. The sound of metal ringing with each swing echoed throughout the training yard as we stepped around each other, and our blades bounced off one another as we circled and evaded the blows we exchanged.

At the last step, as his blade hit mine once more, he stopped his advance. He lifted his blade from mine, lowering it to his side, and he smiled down at me. "Good, good. Your form is getting better. Let's see if your footwork's improved."

He advanced again before I could think, and I ground my teeth together as I braced myself. His sword spun lithely in his hand before he swung it from the right, and I parried swiftly, stepping back.

—Of Shadow and Moonlight

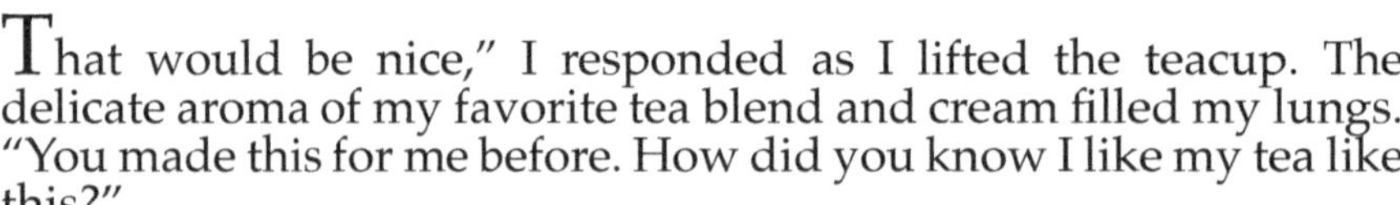

"That would be nice," I responded as I lifted the teacup. The delicate aroma of my favorite tea blend and cream filled my lungs. "You made this for me before. How did you know I like my tea like this?"

He settled into his seat and sipped his coffee. "For the same reasons you know Elena and Lucia."

I blinked at that statement, and for a moment, something like unease churned in my gut at the acknowledgement of the two women who were starting to haunt me. The unease melted away, though, as he ran his fingers through a loose strand of hair, pushing it behind my ear. I caught a glimpse of Ethel smiling over her shoulder, watching him look at me. My chest swelled at the look of endearment on her face, how genuinely happy she seemed to see him like this. It warmed me even more.

He pressed his lips to my temple before setting back in his chair. "Now, eat."

—Of Shadow and Moonlight

Mea paios." *My child.*

An ethereal voice echoed out through the stone hall, a thick accent rolling off her tongue, and I froze. I didn't know the language she spoke, but the voice sounded familiar to me somehow. The moment the strange language spilled from her lips, the voice reached into my mind, speaking in words I understood.

I lifted my eyes to the back of the huge chamber. The starry sky seemed to part to reveal a crescent shape moon carved out into the stone ceiling, letting the moonlight shine down, casting a glow down onto an altar. A pair of large stone horse statues, so intricately carved, they could come to life at any moment, stood merged into either side of the altar's pedestal. Furious energy was carved into their manes and muscles, as if they were charging into battle but frozen in time. Sitting atop the altar between them was a woman, arms draped on either side as she watched us from on high.

She didn't look much older than me, her skin like untouched porcelain and just as pale. Glimmering constellations danced across her nose and cheeks like freckles, and her pale, silver eyes shined like the reflecting gaze of a nocturnal animal in the darkness. A watercolor of shimmering white and silver hair cascaded over her shoulders, spilling like a waterfall over the edges of the stone pedestal where she sat. She didn't glow in the way a light did; it was as if she absorbed all the surrounding light and reflected it off her very being.

As if she were the moon itself.

—Of Shadow and Moonlight

A flood of last-minute instructions spilled from Damien's lips. "We need to know where Marcus and his group went, what they're up to, but don't linger too long. Anything you can get will be good. If you can't find anything, we can try again later."

I took Cole's head in my hands, closing my eyes as I focused on where we connected. It didn't take long before I felt it, as if something were pulling me in. Reaching out to whatever it was, I allowed it to guide me.

My head fell back, muscles spasming and locking up as a wave of thoughts, emotions, and memories invaded me harder, faster than they had with Damien. So many memories, too many at once. Air caught in my throat as my mind was assaulted. Images of Cole's thoughts danced across my mind, visions of his mother taking him for ice cream, of him and his parents laughing at the dinner table.

—Of Shadow and Moonlight

The rich smell of a sweet smoke, like a cigar, wafted into the entry as I reached the foot of the stairway. That same smell had faintly lingered on Damien since I first met him, mixed with his musky scent of cedar and leather, but I'd never smelled it so strongly as I did now. Voices echoed down the hallway, and the smell and conversations grew stronger as I approached the living room.

When I peeked in from the hall, I found Damien standing near the fireplace. Thick smoke rolled from his lips, his hand holding the roll of whatever he smoked just inches from his face.

His amber and ashen eyes lit up when he caught sight of me, and my heart fluttered. "How're you feeling, *mea luna*?"

The conversation died down at his acknowledgement of my presence.

—Of Shadow and Moonlight

From the crowds emerged a woman, her eyes searching the room. In that moment, my heart fluttered in my chest at her presence, something tugging deep within me toward her, but it wasn't my heart that raced. It was Damien's.

She was dressed in the most intricate gown, unlike the rest, though just as beautiful, if not more. Layers of flowing, dusty blue fabric pooled at her feet, her bustier splitting above her breasts, stretching out into long draping sleeves before meeting again around her neck. Her delicate hands grabbed hold of the front of her gown, lifting her skirt as she hurried toward me.

Her eyes were like moonstone, near glittering in the rays of sunlight. Sections of her near silver hair were pulled back into complex braids, draping over the rest of the curls that reached past her hips. I knew her face immediately as she grew closer.

It was me… Or, it was me in a past life.

She smiled up at me, and she positively glowed. "Come on, Damien. You'll not get out of gracing me with at least one dance this night."

I heard Damien's voice as we were dragged forward, a hint of humor on his tongue as we spoke. "I think you've had a little too much to drink, Princess."

"Nonsense. You've had too little," she chuckled, dragging us into the crowd.

—Of Shadow and Moonlight

Y ou were at some party. I saw… me, I think. I wanted a… dance…" The room spun, Damien splitting into two... three... four, and I frowned, blinking as I swayed.

What...

"Cassie?" Damien jumped to his feet, hands on me as he steadied me before I could fall from the chair.

The taste of copper filled my mouth, and something warm rolled over my lips, dripping down my chin and into my lap. I lifted my hand to touch the warm liquid dripping from my nose, and my gaze fell to my fingertips, tipped in blood. My mind hazed over, thoughts struggling to form, my lips failing to form words to speak.

Blood? Why was I...

—Of Shadow and Moonlight

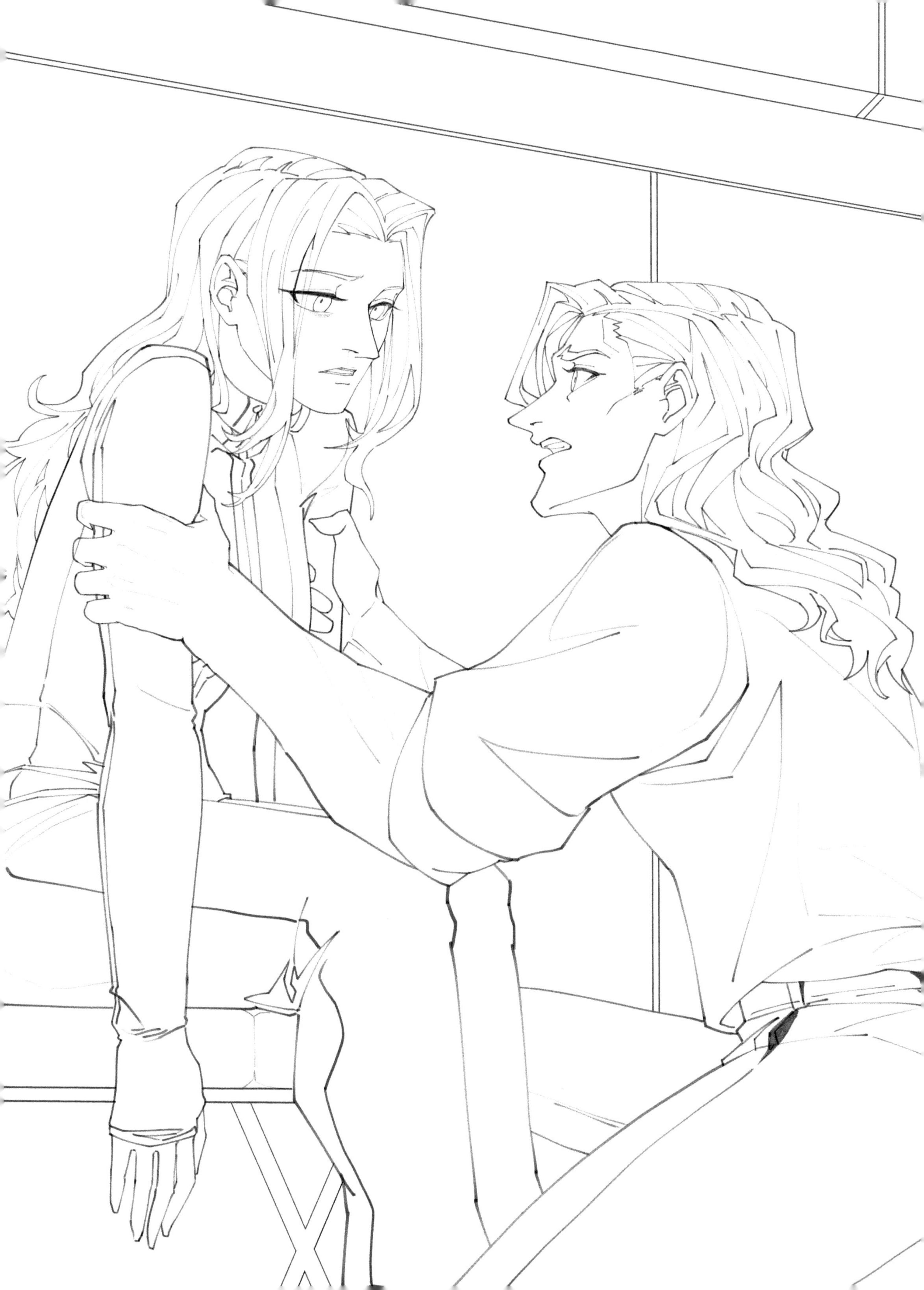

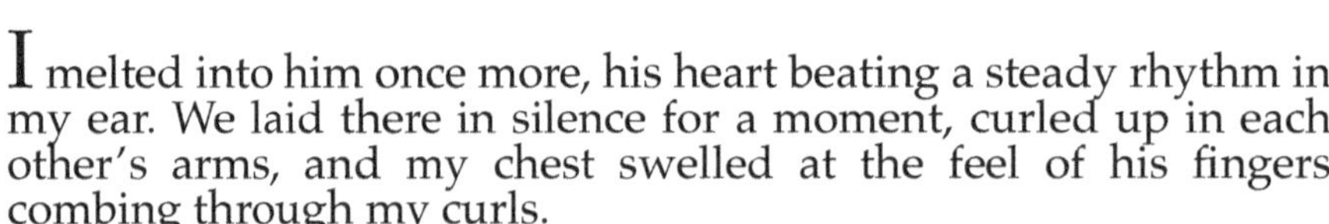

I melted into him once more, his heart beating a steady rhythm in my ear. We laid there in silence for a moment, curled up in each other's arms, and my chest swelled at the feel of his fingers combing through my curls.

"I want you there when it happens," he muttered.

I hesitated a moment, unsure of how I'd feel to see him with another woman like that. Even though he swore there was no intimacy for him, it stung. I wished I could be the one he used, but it was clear it wouldn't benefit him. I curled tighter against him.

"If that's what you want, I'll be there, at your side."

—Of Shadow and Moonlight

Before I knew what I was doing, I was up off the couch. My hand knotted in her hair as I jerked her head back, my other hand tearing my dagger from its sheath, before pressing the blade to her throat. She gasped, her eyes popping open as I held her down, my face inches from hers.

Something had come over me, my body moving as if it wasn't my own. Realization dawned on me as words formed on the tip of my tongue, words that weren't my own. Moira, Elena, and Lucia spoke through me, their wills manifesting in my flesh centuries after their deaths. A strange, overwhelming possessiveness consumed me, and I had to stop myself from slicing the blade across her throat.

I didn't know what language passed through my lips—I only knew what they meant as I spoke through gritted teeth.

"Touen estin emós."

He is mine.

—Of Shadow and Moonlight

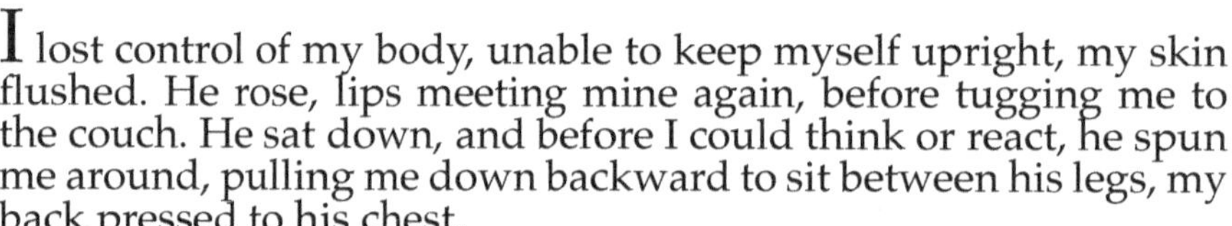

I lost control of my body, unable to keep myself upright, my skin flushed. He rose, lips meeting mine again, before tugging me to the couch. He sat down, and before I could think or react, he spun me around, pulling me down backward to sit between his legs, my back pressed to his chest.

His fangs sank into my neck again, and my back arched, but his hands came around me, one rising to my throat, holding me in place, the other moving down my stomach. A groan of impatience escaped his lips as he fumbled with the buttons of my jeans before he finally got them free, and I cried out at the stroke of his fingertips against my heated flesh.

—Of Shadow and Moonlight

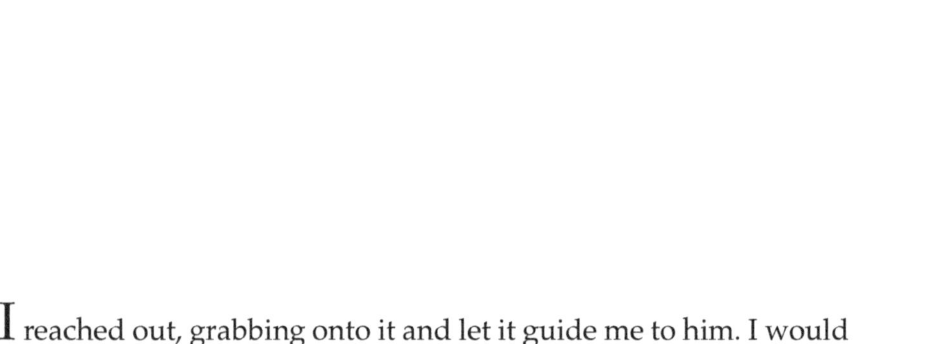

I reached out, grabbing onto it and let it guide me to him. I would only get one shot at this. I had to be quick. There was no telling what would happen if he discovered me.

Images flittered before me, tarnished and shredded, images of Vivienne, the memories slowly deteriorating before me.

He doesn't deserve your pity.

I winced at the voice, at the truth in those words. He didn't, and I held no pity for the monster regardless. I shoved through the reminder of the past, of who he was before he'd lost his mate, and I searched. The images around me shuddered, and something pressed on me, as if the walls were closing in around me.

Shit.

Had he realized I was here? That something was wrong?

—Of Shadow and Moonlight

What do you want with us?" I shouted, shoving down the fury boiling within me.

A crazed grin spread across his face. "To send a message." I stiffened. "This is a revolution, a declaration that we won't be Selene's pawns any longer—won't bury any more of our kind for her mistakes."

Her mistakes? My chest heaved as he grew closer, and my lips parted to speak. "It wasn't her fault what happened to Vivienne!"

The grin slid from his face, his eyes darkening, and I gasped as his hand wrapped around my throat. His fangs slid free as he bared them, his teeth grinding together.

"Don't you dare say her name," he growled. "You know nothing."

I didn't stop, and I was foolish for it, but the words kept coming through quick gasps of air. "You're the one... who made the decision to go! It was your fault!" I gasped as his grip tightened, my mouth opening to speak, but no oxygen came, and I choked out the words. "You want someone to blame? Look... in the mirror!"

—Of Shadow and Moonlight

My body moved involuntarily, some invisible entity coiling around my limbs, guiding me as I stepped into the fire. The flames sparked, rising in a great pyre around me, the power incredible and terrifying. Instinctively, I breathed deeply, as if I were inhaling it into myself, filling my lungs with the heat, the power.

Damien's eyes went wild when he found me, and he howled in horror. "Cassie!"

I couldn't understand what was happening as my body moved on its own, hatred consuming me, rage filling me to the brim. The only fuel that filled me now was the need to get to Marcus, to end him once and for all.

No more. No more would he torment us. No more would he torment *me*. I didn't care what happened to me in the process.

The flames enveloped me in their embrace as the pyre flowed into my body, disappearing from the ground. Heat swarmed every inch of my body, burning yet not burned. My heart raced, its warning one I should heed, but I ignored it, too lost to the fury raging out of control.

—Of Shadow and Moonlight

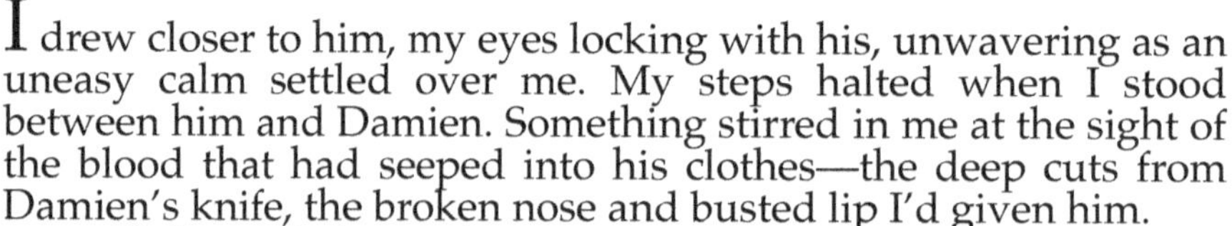

I drew closer to him, my eyes locking with his, unwavering as an uneasy calm settled over me. My steps halted when I stood between him and Damien. Something stirred in me at the sight of the blood that had seeped into his clothes—the deep cuts from Damien's knife, the broken nose and busted lip I'd given him.

He hasn't had enough.

"Not nearly enough," I mused, eyes lifting to Marcus' as Damien stood frozen at my back.

The voice grew stronger in my head, the hate, the anger, the pain he caused me swelling in my chest. It was like a choir of malice in my mind, pushing me over the ledge.

Burn him. Burn him. Burn him. BURN HIM!

My hand slid up against his chest, and I saw my skin for the first time against his bloodied shirt. Veins of hot coals stretched out across my hands and arms, and my skin glowed white. The flames I'd absorbed writhed under my flesh, and red loomed at the fringes of my sight. I couldn't control myself, couldn't stop myself.

Do it now!

—Of Shadow and Moonlight

As he grew closer, his eyes drifted over me, seeming to take in every detail, every bruise, every cut, scrape, and burn that lingered on my skin, every reminder of the man I'd murdered. Faster than I was prepared for, he was within reach of me, his hands coming up but stopping before he touched me.

"*Mea luna?*" Those simple words set loose a sob in my throat, my lips quivering as tears dotted my eyes, and I crumbled.

He pulled me into a deep embrace, as if I were a breath of fresh air and he'd been suffocating. I held onto him as I failed to hold the tears at bay, and he pressed his face into my hair, breathing deeply.

"I'm so sor—" He covered my mouth with his, and I grasped onto his shirt, pulling him closer to me. He only broke the kiss to cup my face, pressing his forehead against my own.

"No apologies. None," he said, his gaze darting back and forth between my eyes before he kissed me again.

—Of Shadow and Moonlight

Damien Archonis, King of The Immortals,
Lord of Shadows… and pancakes.

Seconds after my boots met the damp earth, I turned to launch myself at him once more, and he took an uneasy step back as he lifted his dagger, barely blocking my blow again. I smiled at him, and it seemed to catch him off guard as he frowned.

Perfect.

I shifted my weight away from him, and he stumbled forward. He grunted as I kicked my foot out, hooking his ankle, and pulled it out from under him, my body nearly faltering as well, before I caught myself. His grip loosened as he stumbled, and my free hand shot out, grabbing the guard of his dagger. I twisted, pulling it from his hold as I spun around until I faced him once more, both daggers secure in my grasp, the plastic blades halted against his bare throat.

His chest heaved, his hands rising in quiet surrender as I stared into his eyes. "You've been watching Thalia."

"She's pretty talented at fighting off numerous larger attackers," I said between panted breaths. "I figured I'd take notes."

—Tipped in Frost and Blood

My arms were yanked from my sides, the chains ringing in my ears, the sound too painful to bear. They grew tighter, pulling my arms so hard I thought they might be torn from my body. I gasped as the shadows receded, replaced with concrete walls.

Prisoner.

I pulled against the chains, terror sweeping over me, and for a moment my lungs failed to work. My chest heaved as I tried to breathe. I couldn't breathe, couldn't get free, couldn't... breathe. I couldn't breathe. My eyes widened. No. No, no, no, no, no.

Prisoner.

"This is where you belong, little songbird."

My gaze snapped up to find Marcus before me, his lips curved into the cruel grin that haunted me. His body erupted in flames, and I jerked back, crying out as he closed in on me. His hand shot out, fire coating his skin, and the scent of burning flesh filled my nose as he wrapped his fingers around my throat. The flames grew into a great pyre, eager to devour us. I screamed as it spread over my skin, burning me as the fire consumed every inch of my body.

Murderer.

—Tipped in Frost and Blood

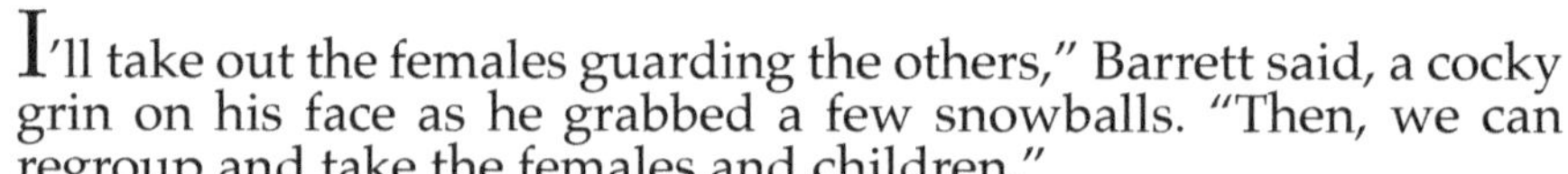

I'll take out the females guarding the others," Barrett said, a cocky grin on his face as he grabbed a few snowballs. "Then, we can regroup and take the females and children."

"Godsdammit, Barrett. You've wasted half of them! Aim better," Zephyr growled, moving what remained of his stockpile out of his reach.

"Why don't you actually throw them instead of stockpiling them?" Barrett bit back before grabbing another, and I wondered if it was just to spite him, which was confirmed when Barrett threw it without looking or aiming. "Is that a shifter thing? Do you bury your food too?"

Zephyr rolled his eyes before turning his back to him, blockading his snowy projectiles.

—Tipped in Frost and Blood

H ere," I said, holding it out to her.

She hesitated a moment before she took the box from my hand. "Is this..."

I nodded, and her eyes lit up before she lifted the lid. For a moment, I saw Elena standing before me, beaming like she had when I'd given her the ornament. Lucia's eyes had lit up the same way when I'd presented it to her our first Solstice together after I found her again. Time could stop, and I almost wished it would, just so I could be lost in this moment with her.

Tears dotted her eyes as she reached into the box and looped her fingers into the ivory ribbon she'd tied to it over seven hundred years ago. Time had left no marks on the carved crystal, the etchings of crescent moons and delicate swirls of the wings glittering still.

She lifted the ornament, allowing it to dangle from her fingers, the crystal coming to life in the fire's glow. "It's as beautiful as I remember it," she whispered, a single tear rolling down her cheek.

I stepped closer to her, pressing a kiss to her forehead as she ran her hand over her cheek, brushing away the tear. "Anywhere?"

I nodded to the tree. "Wherever you like."

—Tipped in Frost and Blood

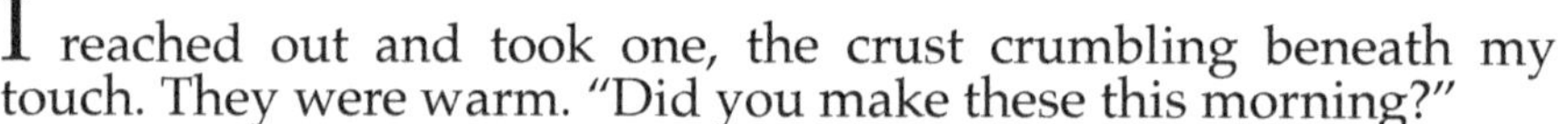

I reached out and took one, the crust crumbling beneath my touch. They were warm. "Did you make these this morning?"

She nodded eagerly. "I've been up since six making them. I wanted to surprise you."

Gods, did she even sleep? I'd gotten in around four, and she'd been pacing the hallway when I arrived.

I took a bite, and my eyes slid shut as the sweet and tart filling met my tongue. Gods, it was just as I remembered, the crust buttery and flakey with just the right amount of crunch before it gave way to the soft, chewy center. She'd told me she loved to bake, and I wondered if a part of her remembered how to make them, because there was nothing that compared. It was the same.

"Damien?" she said, a look of worry painting her face, and I realized tears were rolling down my cheeks.

"Sorry," I said, brushing them away. "I... I haven't had one of these since the last time she made them for me. I would've been... eleven? Twelve, maybe?"

—Tipped in Frost and Blood

ABOUT THE AUTHOR

LUNA LAURIER is the Amazon and Barnes & Noble's Bestselling debut author of Of Shadow and Moonlight. She lives in the south with her husband and son on their little farm. She has a Bachelor's in Business, and when she's not writing you can find her reading, filming cheesy book humor and bookish cosplay Tiktoks, and buying more books when she already has more than she can read.

Tiktok.com / @authorlunalaurier
Instagram.com / authorlunalaurier
Facebook.com / authorlunalaurier
www.lunalaurier.com

ABOUT THE ARTISTS

HUANGJA is a hobbyist and self-taught freelance artist based in Indonesia. She has worked with Luna on the official illustrated scenes in the shadow and moonlight series since its debut in 2022.

Instagram.com / huangja
https:// www.fiverr.com / huangja

VHEXI is a Minnesota based illustrative tattoo artist who also works in digital art, commissioning artwork on the side. She has worked with Luna on the official tattoo designs as well as other select graphics in the shadow and moonlight series since its debut in 2022.

Instagram.com / vhexi

DISCOVER MORE OF THE SHADOW AND MOONLIGHT SERIES BY LUNA LAURIER

A woman fated to die young, a man cursed to live forever, and a darkness that threatens to destroy everything they love.

| book 1 | book 1.5 winter novella | book 2 | book 2.5 / barrettxthalia duology #1 |

learn more...

available on amazon, kindle unlimited, barnes & noble, books-a-million, and wherever books are sold. Signed copies available.